Split In Time

Leisa F. Green

Cover Artwork: by Leisa F. Green

"BiPolar" 16x22 Acrylic on Oval canvas,

December 26, 2018

LeiByDesign

Leisa F Green

5533 Highway 71 South

Cove, Arkansas, 71937

https://www.facebook.com/leisa.fay.green

Acknowledgements

Thank you for the beginning inspiration for this book to the 8th grade student, Tristan, who I worked with to write an outline for a time traveler short story, who then asked that I write my own version of the story for extra motivation while writing his own version.

Thank you for motivating the incredible depth of sensory experiences which stem from personal experiences with a family member. The experiences we have gone through in the past 17 years guided my words in the development of this story and created within me the urge to share and enlighten others to the actuality of these experiences, as well as the patience and understanding that are necessary to survive these experiences.

Thank you to the greatest woman I know for the drive to have this work published, my mother, Shirley. She has always been a wonderful, supportive woman who is my role model for being a good Christian. My three sisters, Nancy, Sheila, and Connie, who instilled in me the drive to follow my heart and reach for my dreams while staying grounded in life. I have much appreciation and love for my best friend and confidante, Beverly, for always pushing me to become a better version of myself and believing in me when I didn't believe in myself. Without these strong and faith filled women and family members in my life, I wouldn't have been able to brave publishing this book.

I also want to show appreciation for my fellow teachers and colleagues at our small school, who are an irreplaceable second family, for their valuable advice and encouragement. And last but certainly not least, my students... Each and every student that I have had, do have, and will have had the immense pleasure of serving in my classroom for inspiring me to grow as an educator. I love them all, past, present, and future.

The Beginning of the End

As I resist awakening from a deep, dream filled sleep, the sweet smell of fresh coffee drifts into my reality. The automaker gurgles with the final droplets of water seeping through its coils, my eyelids feel like concrete slabs; heavy to open and gritty as well. I open them to a soft purple and green haze; this place, this time ...is magical as long as you are inside a structure, toxic if you are not. The haze may seem whimsical from inside this safe cocoon of a time ship, but the air is acidic, sour and deadly.

Stretching out muscles to awaken all my senses, I climb from my pod and step into the auto-dresser, choosing to go with a 1960's theme. Fresh attire attained, comfortable bell-bottoms with a tie-dye top, complete with leather moccasins, acquired during a recent trip to *Earth 1965*. Feeling frisky, I let Margie (the ships bio-intelligent system) choose my morning sustenance. Something new to me from that *Earth 1965* hippie menu.....pancakes with syrup? A side of bacon?... The smell is intriguing! Sweet yet salty, soft and moist, yet crunchy ...yes, I could definitely have lived comfortably in that time and place.

Now that my belly is full, I can think,; it's time to plan an agenda for the day. What shall I do next? It would be nice to know what this world was like before the mass destruction of *Zenthal.* History logs reveal that it was once a lush and clean planet, with beautiful gardens and crystal clear oceans of water. Hmm, I believe that 66 million years ago, should result in a pre-desolate time and place. The sound of the machine computing a date and setting the needed gears to accomplish this, it sounds like wind chimes......musical ...magical.

I reach excitedly to press the start switch and following the soft click, a loud and unexpected explosion takes place. Feeling as though my head will burst with the shock of the BOOM, I grab it and try to hold it together. It's as though it will break apart and I feel the beginning trickle of blood coming from my ears. Time seems to shudder around me at an ever slowing pace until all is still, quiet, with even the air feeling stagnant.

Attempting to get my bearings, I reach for the control panel, which has been mostly destroyed. The display is showing static only, no readings, no information, nothing. I try desperately to call out to Margie for information, but only a raspy whisper escapes from my vocal chords. There must be more damage to my cranium and upper region than I can feel. Perhaps a numbness is protecting me from the pain that I should be feeling, after surviving such a devastating blast.

Wait...I did survive, right? This is more than a mere dream. It has to be! Pull it together!! While searching for liquid, preferably coffee, but water will do, as a way to clear the dryness from my throat, I need to speak with Margie; I need to know that she wasn't damaged, or worse, extinguished. In the distance, I can hear a rustling. Is there a fire somewhere in the ship? Are there creatures beginning to breach the ship? I train my hearing to the sound, focusing on the small rustling and move carefully closer to where the sound appears to be coming from. Wait! That is a moan! There is a person on board with me; someone who had to have been on the ship when it exploded! A stowaway!

I carefully move closer to the intruder, carefully, even though I believe them to be injured or trapped. I notice a hand, five fingers; yes, it appears to be human. From the deep tones of the voice, that sounds to be only moans, I would venture to guess it is a man. Covered with debris from the blast, only a hand and a voice are apparent. Should I try to help him? Should I begin an effort to rescue him from the debris? Uncover the stowaway? Think about it carefully now, Joe, he could be the one who caused the explosion. This could have been an attempt to kill me... destroy my ship... or Margie.

These thoughts didn't last more than a millisecond. This was a living being who was hurt and trapped. No matter the reason for him being there, I have to help him...save him. It would be the only way I would be able to sleep at night, knowing that I had done everything in my power to save him; the only way to find out if he was the cause of it all.

While moving debris I realize some extremely heavy, sharp, and hot remains is piled on top of him, and fires from the sparking electrical wires are all obstacles to overcome, I find myself wondering. Curious thoughts and questions race through my mind. Who is this? How did he gain entry onto my ship, get through all of the security measures. How, on *Zenthal*, did he manage to get past Margie, with all of the security measures that I programmed into her?

All of these questions and more will have to wait to be answered; wait until I have uncovered the unknown male, tended to his wounds and awakened him. I will begin interrogation as soon as he is conscious. Then what? What if he is the one who caused the explosion; what would I do next? Take punitive measures? And to what end?

As I strain to move the last and largest chunk of metal refuse off the unknown man, I get a strange sensation that I know this person already. The familiarity of the structure of his face and jaws are uncovering a long hidden memory.

I, as a child, was happy and content to play with the electronics that were lying around, creating new toys and wonders and as an only child, I had a few deep and serious conversations with... myself. I even went so far as to give my alter-ego his own, unique, name; I called my him 'Ralph' and he was my best and only friend. With no other children on the planet other than myself, he and I were always working side by side, discussing my inventions with enthusiastic consideration of my experimental devices and intentions for them.

Brainstorming with Ralph had helped me keep my sanity, that is until the day that Ralph voiced an opposing opinion. He didn't like the direction I was going with my newest creation. He argued that it was impossible, even insane, to believe that I could create a machine that could carry me through time and space. How little faith he had in me!!!

Ralph and I argued without end for days, until finally his rage grew out of control and he attacked me. It seemed to be drawn out, in slow motion, powerful, and a particularly violent battle. Fist to face, knee to torso, blow upon blow, and a final choke hold that ended with a shocking separation. We....we physically tore... apart.

It was as though we were made of rubber that was being stretched to the point of breakage. Fine, taut strands pulling past their limits, and then... the separation sounded like fingernails on a chalkboard, paper being ripped in half, a piercing sound followed by a sudden and deafening silence. No longer were we Joe; we were now Joe... and Ralph. I... had been torn, split in time, and now felt utterly incomplete.

As Ralph walked away from the battle zone, bruised and limping, I watched him slowly leave me. My breathing became slower, calmer, and I then realized in that moment that I was free... free from conflict over my inventions, free from arguing, and yet I felt alone...

Many years have passed since that fateful day and I have become accustomed to being alone, except for Margie. Oh Margie, what a sanity saver that ingenious bit of technology. Created out of desperation for companionship, Margie has become my one ally. M (mobile) A (artificial) R (real-time) G (gateway) I (intelligence) E (emulation). I don't believe I would have retained any semblance of sanity without her over the last 100 or so years. But now, is she still functional?

I won't know until I get some of this cleaned up, until I figure out what is wrong with her system and repair it. However, first, I must uncover the unknown being and try to get to some answers about exactly what happened.

With the last of the debris moved from atop the humanoid, I can see that, yes, this is a familiar face. Although bloody and bruised, I can clearly see the profile of ...Ralph! That would explain his undetected entry to the ship. We once were one, therefore we share identical DNA, look almost exactly the same, and our voices are indistinguishable. Margie would not have been able to discern between Ralph and I; she could never have detected the slightest difference as the only sense that she cannot replicate is sight. His hair is white and very short and neat, whereas mine is long, pitch black and wavy. Along with a few scars obtained in the last couple of centuries, the pale, gaunt skin tone and a goatee, we are identical in structure, stature, and facial features.

My heart skips a beat and I am riveted, staring blankly at the form in front of me. He seems unconscious, but I am wary. I quickly scan the immediate area for something of substance that can be used to tie his hands and feet. After the last bout of rage that I experienced with him, I am unsure of how he will respond when he wakes up.

Finding only loose wires hanging from the electronics on the ship, I quickly use a red one to tie his hands and feet. I try to make the bindings secure, yet not tight enough to cause pain or discomfort. He was a part of me once, the last thing I want to do is harm him. I place a folded curtain under his head and leave him to awaken on his own.

Cleaning up is going to take a while. As I gather some of the larger debris and place it into bins, I mentally keep a record of items that need repair and those that are unsalvageable. The technology that can't be repaired without specialty parts is adding up. They can't be made from common items on the ship, or from 66 million years or who knows how long ago in this unfamiliar place. I will need to explore soon, to search for and find resources.

It occurs to me, now, that I haven't taken the time to explore outside of the ship in any way whatsoever. First, to clean up as much as I can. At least then, when I do find resources to use in repairing the ship, I will have a tidy place to organize them.

Several hours have gone by since the crash and judging by the shadow play visible through the cracks that are in the ship's hull, it now seems to be getting dark outside. My 'guest' has yet to regain consciousness and I am beginning to wonder if he will any time soon. I sit and write on an old paper, taking stock of what is necessary in order to begin the repairs. Wow, it has been eons since I have done this and I am a bit rusty, but it feels good to get something planned in a visual format.

As I list the areas of the ship that need work in an order of importance, draw diagrams, note instructions for each needed repair, and make material lists, I notice that my guest begins to slightly stir. He whispers but one word, "Thirst". I take a water bladder out of the bin and put it up to his mouth. He barely swallows any, never even opens his eyes, and then immediately drifts back off. Well, OK. I guess he's going to live afterall.

To Be and To Do

The mechanical doors are extremely heavy and slightly warped from the explosion, making it near impossible to pry them open. With a heavy metallic groan, the doors inch apart; a dark fog begins to seep into the ship. Should I reverse, close the doors, and retreat back to the safety of being inside the ship? No, it would be certain doom to remain inside without the supplies that I need to repair the ship. I would slowly suffocate when the air ran out or starve or even go mad from being confined with…him. I continue to pry apart the doors to find a dense, glowing fog swirling heavily around the ship. I can make out rudimentary shapes of possibly tropical plants. The temperature is close to unbearable; the fog, sticky and warm. The taste in my mouth is salty, almost as if the planet were sweating. I step out into the foggy atmosphere and instantly a slimy tentacle like appendage brushes against my calf and twitches……as if it were having a seizure-like episode. I can only imagine that it is delighting in the flavor of my leg.

The green glow of the mist before me creates an eerie ambience, like being in a haunted graveyard with the dead rising from the grave to capture my life force. Pull it together, Joe. It's just a forest in the middle of nowhere, no dead rising, and no monsters coming. Just you, this stench of a fog and a few sightless and toothless, muzzled helminths writhing on the surface, in search of something to eat. Yet, the fear creeps up my spine and makes the little hairs on my neck stand out like a flower reaching for sunlight.

As I begin to stumble over some unseen lump on the surface, I reach out for an anchor to hold me upright and grab onto one of the tropical...esque plants. A viscous ooze encases my skin, like it is trying to absorb me. A deep and thorough shiver runs the length of my entire body to the point that I feel as though I will pass out or purge my pancakes at any second. Desperately trying to avoid any more of the sticky substances, I feel down the shaft of the plant to locate a dry and uncoated area to hang onto. But as I do, something even slimier inches across my hand. It's really hard not to scream, but I am anxious about making any loud noises because I am unsure of what is actually out there in the glowing fog and darkness.

Noises, some clear and others barely audible as if creatures big and small are moving about, are feeding my anxiety. A loud and distinct clicking in a rhythmic pattern, repeats itself first to the left of me, then, to the right as though two indigenous insects were discussing, maybe even planning, to interact with the new species....me.

Interact in what way, though? Hopefully friendly. Then above my head, I hear a chittering, reminiscent of a spider monkey or an audio of spider monkeys from Earth in the 21st century. Occasionally, there is a high pitched scream that causes my muscles to tense, my hair to stand on end, and my breathing to stop momentarily. How am I going to overcome this overwhelming fear of the unknown? If only the sun would rise and give light to this world. Ok, maybe there is no sun rising, but without any light source it seems I will wander aimlessly in the dark forever..........

The ground disappears from beneath my feet and in an instant I am falling into an ever darkening void, floating it seems, into nothingness. It is as if I have fallen into a bottomless pit of darkness. Although I am grasping desperately and repeatedly, there is nothing to grab onto to stop the fall. The only tangible sense besides the sensation of falling is the horrid stench. It is sour and rotten, as if many dead or dying things have gathered at the bottom of this pit to decay. Please ...don't let me join that gathering........

Time seems to have come to a standstill as I effortlessly and endlessly float downward, nothing to stop my decent, nothing to give a hint as to how deep this crevice is, and no hint of what is to come, except the increasing stench of decay.

Someday, in the distant future, an exploration party will find my remains. Six feet in length, thin and sinewy, mummified remains with tufts of black hair scattered randomly upon the scalp. They will wonder about the moments before my death. Did I feel fear? Pain? The sticky goo that I am embedded in, was it cold or a heated pot of stinking, snot-like substance? This fall is leaving way too much time for thoughts. I wish it would
. . . .

Landing was NOT as expected, almost like a floating feather coming to rest on a soft grassy carpet. All the anxiety quickly drips from my body and I relax. It is warm in temperature, but not too warm with a soft violet glow illuminating the walls of this cavern. Stalactites and stalagmites are visible in the distance just a few paces forward. And the smell has suddenly become pleasant... smoky almost, as if someone is toasting marshmallows.

Which reminds me, I have had nothing to eat since pancakes. It seems like hours ago. The rumbling of my stomach echoes around the cavern, like a spirit looking for a way out. The search for food becoming more urgent, I move towards the glow. I realize it isn't what I left the ship in search of. But not knowing how long it will take me to find my way back, it is important to feed the dragon when he growls, so that he doesn't become too angry and cause me to lose consciousness.

Having traveled to many galaxies and through many periods of time, I have ingested lots of unusual things, some tasty, others not so palatable. But, the important thing is that it is filling and provides the energy needed to continue the search for materials to repair my ship.

So far, I have seen no other intelligent life to question about food sources or materials, so it is important to be suspicious of every possible morsel. The further I go, the more interesting become the plants I can see hanging from the walls or sprouting from the mossy carpet below my feet; fruits are apparent on some and hidden beneath nutty shells on others. I should be gathering, so I look around for something to hold the possibly edible foodstuffs.

Finding a seemingly woven netting that is drooping sporadically from the ceiling of the cave and using the only tools that I have on me, a pair of cutting tools called a Westcott, similar to scissors, and a carving tool which resembles a knife with a curved and scooped blade that I call a Wusthof hook-knife, I cut sections of the organic netting before tying the corners to form a bag shape that I can hoist over my shoulder as I wander through the rest of the cave.

First, I gather a good amount of soft spherical fruits, of which the colors range from a bright green to a deep ocean blue. They have a sweet and tangy aroma, so they are very tempting. As I move through the cave, there are several leafy vines hanging about, like ropes, from outcroppings of huge rocks. Shall I? I think I shall......attempt to use one of the sturdier looking vines as a rope to climb up to the face of one of the outcroppings and explore what might be up there.

Feeling a bit weak from hunger, I decided first to eat one of the pungent fruit that I have already collected and drank some water that had been caught in a curved leaf as it drips endlessly from the ceiling of the cave. It's cold and refreshing and tastes very clean. Now, the fruit. With the first bite, I am overcome with exhilaration. It is juicy and succulent, tasting much like an Earth fruit, a peach, light but sweet and filling.

With my stomach, now settled and satisfied, I begin my ascent. Wrapping the vine around my thigh and ankle for leverage, I reach above my head to get a tight grasp of the ropelike vine and move my way upward by pulling upwards then readjusting the vine around my ankle to push forward again in order to grasp even higher. Taking only a few minutes to accomplish my goal, I reach the edge of the outcropping and pull myself onto the shelf, which I find to be flat and dry. By the light emitted from glowing moss on the back edge of the rock cliff, I can see some small fungi-like, wispy and luminous mushrooms. The iridescent, angry pink puffs look quite dangerous, yet particularly inviting all at the same time. I gently pluck one from where it is growing and it snaps off, sounding somewhat like a dry twig.

A sweet aroma drifts through the air, exquisite and savory, creating a new sense of enormous craving. In the whole of my 300 year life span, I have never wanted anything more desperately than I do right now. I am not hungry, my belly is quite satisfied and yet I feel as though I will cease to exist if I am denied the pleasure of tasting this succulent treat.

As I place the bulbous top of the mushroom into my mouth, it is as if I have been transported into another world; a world filled with pleasure and emotion. Floating weightlessly in colorful sparkling clouds of dust and sweetness, I feel free and more alive than ever before. No longer deprived of the knowledge of the universe, but filled with knowledge of all; satiated to the point of divine, everlasting, and infinite knowledge; immortal and celestial, I am now all-seeing.

I see myself as if I were not I. Lengthy and lanky, skin as of tanned leather, my coal black hair and eyes stare back at me with wonder. A creature appears, at first just a glow with flowing tentacle like appendages, then more clearly. It isn't moving closer, it is just...materializing before my eyes. The face is angelic and indescribable, four legged and hairy...soft, wavy fleece of the purest white, powerful and vigorously built, I feel strength radiate from the being.

As I am watching him...become, he moves closer to the other I, the one that I see, as if I am merely an onlooker to the scene before me. Although I hear no words, he is speaking wonders and secrets to my other self. Not merely departing wisdom, but the secrets of the universe, the planet, and me...myself...I.

The celestial being calls itself Bob and seems to not merely transform, but shrink and expand. At first, he seems larger than life, then after what seems like hours of change he is tiny, miniature, fitting in the palm of his hand...my hand... He is whispering loudly, directions, almost as a visual map, of a river of metal that can be transformed into anything.....any ...thing. This mental / visual treasure map is being rolled up and given to him... me and placed in his... my pocket. Soft clouds of silver and gold form under his...my head and Bob snuggles up next to him... me making the most delicate and tiny indention. I can feel myself drifting, see myself relaxing even more.......

Waking from the ....dream? Hallucination? Spiritual journey? I find myself refreshed, happy, and confident, as if I could conquer the universe. Under my head is a silvery pillow of wispy cotton-like material. I see the indentation that was made by my head and just to the left of it, a smaller indention, as if an acorn had been there only moments before. In my right pants pocket is a carrot sized roll of parchment, which I do not recall placing there. As I begin to unroll it, it is larger than a carrot and seems to grow organically, surging and rippling until it comes to rest on the cliff's surface. It is a map to a river with picture instructions for building a portable vessel in which to transport the liquid. I must be missing a chunk of time.....I don't recall drawing this, yet I recognize my own handwriting in the instructions.

Ok, Joe, shake it off and get your head straight. Apparently, you have a plan that seems viable in the quest to find materials for fixing the ship. Not sure what the liquid is for, but it seems to be the most important material to gather, so let's get started on creating a way to get it back to the ship. I begin the climb back down the vine to the cave floor, keeping an eye out for any sign of a way out of this cave. Just as my second foot touches down, I catch a glimpse of what seems to be roots, coming from the ceiling, so I move in that direction. Where there are roots below a surface, there is also a path through that plant root system to the surface, right?

The roots seem pretty solid and almost resemble tree roots, but how to use this to create a tunnel to the open air? I am totally at a loss on that question. But the roots look a lot like the material that is used in the instructions to create a container to carry liquid. So I retrieve my only two tools from my belt and begin work, first using my Wusthof hook knife to hack at the sizable root until only minute strands of splinters were left binding the two sections together. Then, using the Westcott, I clip the remaining strands and disengage the two sections. Now, after separating two bucket sized sections from the main root, I begin the tedious process of hollowing out the interior with the Wusthof.

It takes more than an hour to complete the task and I am quite worn when it is finally done. Next, I connect the two vessels with a length of vine to use as a strap in carrying them. Okay. It's break time. The need to rest before the search for an exit is imperative, as I could stumble and become incapacitated and unable to continue my quest.

After a short but needed respite, including a tasty fruit snack, I am fully restored and prepared for a tenuous journey. Being very still and listening for any sound to hint at the river on the map, I catch a gurgling sound to my far left. As I hone in on the sound of moving water, I begin walking carefully towards it, carrying the two vessels strapped across my shoulders, hanging at my side just under my grip of the vine that ties the two together.

The sound of the liquid moving deepens and becomes more perceptible the closer I get to it and within only minutes, I can see it. It's as if a waterfall is coming out of the rock face with no perceptible origin visible. The liquid has a shimmer and looks as if it is molten silver. Beautiful fluid motion, rippling slightly as it reaches the small stream beneath, then settles into a slow seductive dance towards the bank of the stream.

As fascinating as the motion of the stream is, I can't stand here all day and gaze at it. Removing the strap from across my shoulder, I set down one root-bucket and take the other to the edge of the stream.

Slowly lowering the side of the bucket, some of the liquid metal begins to run into the carved out interior. You would think that this liquid metal would be extremely hot, but it is cool to the touch, as a bit splashes onto my hand. Once one root bucket fills, I retrieve the other and began filling it with the liquid. I fully expect the liquid to smell metallic and be burning to the touch, but it is cool and gives off a clean, fresh hint of recently cut cocobolo wood.

Time to get this liquid metal back to the ship. It should be perfect for making the components needed to repair electrical and electronic systems. Now, how to get out of this hole?

So far, I haven't noticed any fresh air ports or light beams shining through the ceiling, but then again, I haven't really been looking. I guess it would be wise to focus solely on the task of searching for an escape route, now. There seems to be a slight slope to the ground, heading ever slightly upwards, a sharp contrast to the endless falling that got me here.

After what seems like hours, the air starts to change. It is getting thinner and drier. Hopefully, this is a sign that I am nearing an exit to this cave. It seems as though I have been inside here for days.

I hope that my brother, my prisoner, has not succumbed to thirst and hunger; I never meant to leave him tied up like that for any extended period of time. I don't have it in me to inflict that kind of torture on anyone, even my most feared enemy. But, at least he is out of the elements and away from any harmful or deadly creatures that may inhabit this planet.

Wait a second... I can smell fresh foliage and the air is moving ever so slightly. I am nearing a passage out; light is spilling into the darkness and transforming the iridescent moss into a dark green, dappled with varying shades of orange, wispy fur. Amazing colors and stark changes are taking place before my eyes, as I move towards the light source.

This place is quite magical. Ready to get back to my ship, but hesitant to leave this wonderland, I move slowly and steadily towards the exit point being careful not to spill the contents of the makeshift root-wood buckets.

As I step through the opening of the cave and into the sunlight, I cannot believe my eyes; the ship is within a few feet of me. I can clearly see the glint of the metallic outer hull of it through the cleanly cut pathway that is before me. It looks as though the path was cleared weeks ago and is frequently used, as it is worn cleanly and evenly in a direct line with the ship's position. Had I been gone for eons? Had someone cleared the way and patiently kept it tidy for my return? Nonsense, this could not be!! Putting aside my questions, I move swiftly up the path and with only ten or so strides, I am standing alongside the mechanical doors.

Hoping that there is enough power still in the ship's storage unit to operate the sizeable door, I reach to open it and… to my surprise, it swishes open with ease. There was no scraping metal, no heavy groan… no effort on my part at all. It is as if the ship repaired itself..? Ok, now that's just crazy talk!! Pull it together, Joe! Someone must be awake, unbound, and feeling helpful. It has to be Ralph who worked on the doors.

Setting down my makeshift buckets full of the liquid metal substance, I step inside the ship. Nope, still messy... still broken. And Ralph? Still tied up in the hallway area, with red wire around his ankles and wrists, still sleeping on the folded curtain pillow... snoring loudly. It is as if only minutes had passed since I left him inside, but it had been days. Surely, it had to have been days.

Since all is the same as I left it, well, a bit better than I left it, I will continue gathering the needed supplies to make the parts that will be needed to repair the ship. But first, I really need to figure out how to make this liquid metal become a solid metal, in order to make the parts. I can't just pour it over the broken pieces and expect it to magically transform into a wholly working part; what a silly thought... perhaps light will harden it, heat, or a chemical. I need to set up several experiments to figure out how to alter it to a more malleable material.

Small cups and other supplies located, experiment stations arranged, I now transfer small doses into petite metal containers and get them to the stations. One station is located in direct sunlight to measure any viable change due to sunlight.

A second station, located in a well-vented location, will be used for detecting changes due to adding various chemicals independently, one by one. The last station is located near a fire pit, built by surrounding a small hole, about a foot deep, with large stones that I had found near the ships location. I arrange them around the exterior rim of the hole.

I will need to gather kindling and a few larger pieces of wood in order to get a fire hot enough to test the ability to forge the metal. Before going to gather wood, though, I should set one of the containers of liquid metal on the station that is in direct sunlight in order to give the substance more time to make a possible transformation.

Glancing into the doorway as I pass by after placing the container on the sun shelf, Ralph is struggling to free himself from his restraints. It's time to go in and check on his state of mind. I truly hope he is amiable and cooperative. He doesn't look angry.......

"How are you feeling?"

"Honestly, my head is killing me and I need to pee. Want to explain to me why I have been tied up?"

"You don't remember? Not really surprising based on that enormous knot on your forehead. Let me see if I can locate a compress and some ice, then we can talk about what happened to my ship."

"Any chance you could untie me first? I mean ...I do need to pee quite badly."

He feels cold and clammy to the touch as I untie him. I hope he at least feels bad enough not to try and fight me. Please let him be calm.......

"There you go. Better?"

"Much. Thank you from the bottom of my bladder. Are the amenities functional or shall I go outside and find a tree?"

"The toilet is functional, but fresh air might do you a bit of good."

As we walk outside, Ralph slips off behind a tree to the left of the ship. Looking at it, it is almost as though the ship is healing itself. Odd. Laying on the ground next to the ship's doorway, there are two rather hearty looking straps. Those will surely make gathering firewood less of a task.

"Oh man, I needed that. Another few minutes and I think I would have wet myself." Ralph said with a chuckle. "The air is really sweet here. Where are we?"

"I have no idea, nor do I know *when* we are. All I can tell you is that I have found materials to use in repairing the ship once I figure out how to best use them."

"The ship. All I can remember is a massive noise and hard vibrations then poof..... Nothing until my bladder woke me up about to explode."

"I need to know... How did you come to be on my ship? And why?"

"Do you have any water? I could really use some rehydration. I feel as though I have been out for days."

After retrieving a water for Ralph, he explained to me that he had come to make amends but when he approached the ship, the door scanned him and just opened up, so he came in to the smell of coffee brewing. Before he could locate me, the ship… seemed to implode, for a lack of better words. The blast knocked him backwards and he doesn't remember anything beyond the impact with the inner wall of the ship.

"Talking is good, and you needed some fresh air, but I really need to gather some wood for a fire pit in order to check the forge ability of this substance that I believe is the answer to repairing the ship."

"I can help. I am feeling much more able now. Let me walk with you and help you locate kindling."

Stooping down to retrieve the straps then flinging them over my shoulder, I can see that his clothes are a bit tattered, just as mine are from the ship's mishap. What a rough looking pair we make as we slowly start down the path back towards some broken limbs for kindling that I had spotted earlier... It is only a click away from the ship, so it only takes minutes to reach it.

Removing the straps from my shoulder, I fashioned a sling to use as a backpack in bringing back the cargo. Ralph bends to pick up one and becomes dizzy, weaving slightly.

"Whoa, hold on there buddy! I can pick them up. You place them in my pack, okay? We don't need for you to pass out, out here. I am not sure that I am in a condition to carry you back and I am sure you don't want to be dragged along this path." I said with a touch of humor.

"No, no!! I am already banged up enough. Being dragged through the forest is the last thing I want, right now." He replied.

The pack is full in a heartbeat and we head back towards the ship, down the same path we came on. The pack is heavy with kindling and it feels as though we are moving in slow motion; one leaden foot step after the next, we make slow progress. Although it is only a click away, it seems like miles and I am exhausted before we get there. Ralph goes on ahead and retrieves a water for me, handing it to me just as I reach the pit.

Removing the straps from my shoulders, the branches land with a solid whump! Slumping down onto one of the stones surrounding the pit, I take a deep drag on the water and wipe the dribble from my chin. So refreshing! I was about to start sweating like the planet seemed to be doing when I first left the ship. I wonder what the day cycle is like here. How much of this sunlight do we have left before the hot fog returns? Better get a move on in making this fire.

I lean into the pit to place the branches so that they can get enough air to continually burn at high heat, for an extended time, perhaps all through the night cycle. Ralph hands me one at a time, trying to surmise which one I would need next in order to build a sustainable pit fire that would suffice for forging.

"So… this substance you found. What is it?"

"It's like a liquid metal. It was running in a small stream, hidden deep in a cave. That cave." I point towards the cave entrance… where the cave entrance was? Now, there are only trees and vines. Surely I had not imagined being so close to the ship when I emerged from the cave… This planet seems to be evolving, changing every time I am not looking, in the same way the ship appears to be healing itself.

The branches now in place with a good stack set aside to fuel the fire, I search my pockets for tools to spark it. Finding only a Wusthof, Westcott, and a bit of string, I realize this will not be sufficient to start a fire. Remembering an old video of a situation based survival show, I asked Ralph to find something to use for kindling while I carve out a V shape in a flattened shard of wood to use as a fire board.

When Ralph returns with a double handed size pile of dried mossy vegetation, I pick a few pieces of bark from the stack of branches then build a tinder nest. Once this seems to be adequate, I place a bit of the dried kindling into the V notch next to a small stone, then place the end of one of the quarter round sticks, fashioned to work as a spindle, into the depression on the fireboard, against the edge of the small amount of dried moss and bark.

Working the spindle between my palms, so that it rotates quickly in a twisting motion, to create heat friction. It takes several minutes of this motion to detect a bit of smoke, but as soon as it is evident, I blow gently into the kindling and presto! Flames begin to lick upward through the kindling! Taking care not to lose the flame, I place the small fire into the pit beneath some of the smaller branches and add more of the dried moss, to boost the flames. Within only a few minutes, we have a raging pit fire.

As we relax by the fire, my stomach begins to rumble and it reminds me that I haven't eaten in hours, and it feels like days. "I am starving. What do you say we go inside the ship and scrounge for something to eat?"

We both get up and go inside. Once in the galley area, Ralph spots a container of legumes and a vacuum sealed roll of smoked summer sausage. I locate some unleavened bread squares, I believe they are called crackers, and a small block of aged cheddar. Slicing the sausage and cheese onto a platter, adding a side of squares, then unsealing the legumes, we carry our meager meal outdoors to consume it, by the blazing fire. The legumes are tastier when heated, so I place the can on a warm stone at the edge of the fire.

Remembering the sunlight-affect experiment, I check the liquid metal and observe that there is no noticeable change. We still have fire and chemicals to test, so I am not worried.

As we sit by the blaze, I notice that the light is fading and the fog is returning and it creeps ever closer to the ship, seeming to avoid the heat of the fire, leaving a clear void around us. It seems like an excellent atmosphere for conversation while we wait for the fire to create a bed of coals, suitable for forging metal. Ralph begins the conversation, "Looks like you've accomplished the time travel dream."

"If I hadn't, we wouldn't be in this predicament." I responded in a joking tone.

"How long have you been doing this...? Traveling through time?"

"About fifty years. The places and times I have seen would curl your toes!"

"Have you not been lonely? Having no one to talk to?"

"Oh, on the contrary, my long lost brother, I have not been so alone. Before the ship was in working order, I first developed a companion, a bio-intelligent interface system. Margie, mobile / artificial / real-time / gateway / intelligence / emulation. My most valuable bit of equipment. She truly has been quite a conversationalist at times, is quite handy with informational things, has kept me on my toes with her humor, and has been an integral part of operating the ship. Her repair and resuming online function is paramount to the operation of the ship. My first order of business is to fashion circuits to repair her motherboard and get her operational."

"Do you think she will be able to detect the source of the explosion? I mean, knowing what caused it would, no doubt, be beneficial. If the blast originated from malfunctioning equipment, damage from some foreign object during time-shift, or... could it be possible that Margie is responsible? I mean, this isn't the destination that you programmed, is it? She ultimately controls the time/location of the ship's destination, correct?"

"That is ridiculous! She is only capable of generating from the knowledge that I, MYSELF, programmed into her operating system. That type of defiance would take an ability to independently produce directives and a sense of emotion. That is nonsense, utter nonsense. Once I restore her, she can do a diagnostics scan on the ship's functions prior to, and up to, the impact of the blast, then we can hone in on the defect and repair it, as well as the damage resulting from it."

"We can only know the cause with her help. Is that what you are saying? Return her function, let her determine the reason? Oh my gullible brother, I truly hope that you are right. If she happened to glitch or evolve and become capable of independent thought, and possibly emotion as well, she could also hide her involvement by leading you into a false security, then succeed with her next attempt at total annihilation."

"If it is as you say, what would be her motivation? This is irrelevant… The focus is on repairing the ship to functioning status and figuring out the cause so that viable changes can be done to ensure the future safety of the ship, and its occupants."

The darkness appears as though it is attempting to squeeze out the light of the fire, pushing in then withdrawing with the flickering of the flames. We sit in silence, clearly in disagreement over the possibilities of what caused the ship to malfunction.

Noises coming from the dense undergrowth around us sends a chill up my spine. The rustling in the bushes and from the treetops, humming of insect-like creatures all around, flapping of winged unknown things, and the most disturbing of all, the distinct gurgling and hissing coming from just outside the ring of light that the fire is throwing out is quite disturbing. Anxiously, I poke and feed the fire, causing the blaze to climb higher and brighter, crackling back to life and throwing sparks high into the air.

A loud screech bursts from directly overhead and both Ralph and I quickly jump to our feet, readying to flee into the ship at the first sight of the danger that is stalking us on this strange and peculiar planet. The day-cycle seemed to stretch into several of what I know to be days, what will the night-cycle bring? Will it seem almost endless, as well? Can we sustain the fire throughout an extended night? Will my end come by the unseen slithering creatures that tasted my flesh when I first stepped into the dark undergrowth in my quest for materials? And Ralph, will he survive the night as well or in spite of my questionable fate, or be eaten by unknown creatures that are hungry for a taste of a rare delicacy, as well? My mind continuously racing with dark and ever darkening thoughts as the minutes tick by, every muscle in my body is contracting, as fear seems to soak into every cell of my body.

"Ralph, could you go to the galley area and look for some metal containers, about twice the size of the smaller ones that I have here? I want to see if the heat from the fire is enough to harden the liquid to a more workable consistency." Getting no immediate response, I turn to face him.... He isn't there, just a bare stone where he had sat only moments ago. Did he go inside at my request? Had he already been taken even before I had said anything to him? Or... No. I will not let my mind go in that direction, not without investigation. No conclusions based on my uncontrolled fear.

Attempting to remove the thoughts now racing through my mind, I take a deep breath, lay down my makeshift fire iron and turn to go into the ship into search of Ralph. Everything seems to be in slow motion, now, even the sounds coming from the surrounding forest. High pitch screeching becomes a deeper extended squawking, like a raptor from ancient Earth. The buzzing insect noises become a rhythmic throbbing, flapping wings become heavy drum beats, gurgling becomes growling, hissing rises to unbearable levels just as the winds of a tornado do just before the eye of the storm.

Even as the threshold is only steps away, it seems to take an unbearable, incessant period of time to reach the doorway. Beginning to feel as though I have been holding my breath for hours, about to pass out, blackness starts to inch into the outer edges of my vision, I step into the ship.

It's an instant shift, and an instant relief. Panting and sucking in the air, time suddenly begins passing at what seems to be a normal rate, again. I feel as though I have just been released from a wall of molasses, out of breath, exhausted, relieved...

"Ralph!" I call out and receive no response. Repeat. Nothing. Walking down the corridor towards the galley, I keep calling out, in an increasingly lower volume, each time, beginning to question the safety of calling out. By the time I reach the galley, my voice is but a whisper. Apprehension is now gripping my very soul. I can hear movement coming from behind, so whirling around, thinking I will see Ralph standing there with humor in his eyes at my paranoia, I find nothing. Are the lights flickering ever so slightly? Dimming? Thud! The sound of a cabinet door closing behind me. I whirl around quickly who closed it. No one. Nothing. Nada. Feeling as though someone... or something... is watching my every move, enjoying my transparent fear at the situation. Whispers begin, again, very subtle at first, almost inaudible, then increasingly louder. Can't make out what is being said... tune in on it, focus Joe. Focus!

"They're coming." The disembodied voice whispers, almost as if it were only inches from my right ear. Again, more clearly, "Hurry, you must hurry."

But hurry where? Back outside? To another part of the ship? Hurry in what way? To close the door? To forge the parts needed to repair the ship so that I can get out of here?

Confused and frightened, I frantically search for the items I need to pour the liquid metal in, in order to heat it, hopefully to a workable consistency. Ahh, there they are. I grab three containers - safe for heating at high temperatures and over an open flame, and a medical kit - complete with forceps and tweezers.

Swiftly making my way back down the corridor to the exterior door, I step outside. A sweltering fog surrounds the ship, once again. The creature noises are almost unbearable, but I must keep moving, working to create a substance that can be manipulated into the parts I need. I found a metal syringe in the medical kit along with other tools that can be used for delicate molding tasks. These will be extremely helpful tools in recreating the small circuits needed for Margie's motherboard interface and precisely placing them in the correct positions.

Frequently glancing back over my shoulders, I have to refocus my vision each time, to take in any changes in my surroundings. Just outside the ring of light being cast by the fire, I keep catching tiny movements in my peripheral vision. Flashes, that when I turn to look fully in that direction, they disappear. Figments of my imagination? Perhaps, but better cautious than eaten.

"Let me assist." I hear in my left ear in a raspy whispering voice. Ralph? No. Sounds more feminine. Margie? Impossible, she isn't back online, yet. "Don't do it... Reactivating her is a mistake. She did this. She blew up the ship. She tried to kill you... us... end us..." Definitely not Margie. The whispers are becoming more vivid, clearer, and more frantic. Who is this...? This disembodied voice, this phantom voice. What is this? Why does it 'haunt' me? How can I block it out? Until I can get Margie back online, I cannot get a diagnostic to find out where the blast originated, and cannot diagnose all of the damage. The voice.....keeps persisting.

Through the continual sounds of beasts in the foliage surrounding me, I can hear something... rustling, moving around in the edge of the darkness, just outside of the light. Swoosh! As if an extremely large bird-like being flew over my head. I duck from the sound and feel the wind whoosh through my hair. Whatever it is, it seems to be dive-bombing me, trying to interrupt my efforts.

I desperately try to keep the fire burning bright, having dwindled substantially when I was inside gathering supplies. Containers now filled about three quarters of the way with liquid metal substance then delicately placed on racks and lowered down into the fire while flames are licking the edges, sparks flying when coming in contact with a drip of the liquid on the outer edge of the vessel.

"I can help you." the whisper becoming more cynical, more... dark. "I could guide you if you will only listen!" Can a whisper also be a shout? "You must abandon this insanity, return to the safety of the ship!"

YES! The liquid is changing, evolving, solidifying. It is at a gelatin consistency, a little more and it will be malleable enough to be shaped into circuits. Ignore the voice. Keep focus. Keep working. You can do this, Joe. You ARE the 'Ultimate Time Travel Genius'.

WHAM! Sounding as if a tree has fallen on the ship, I jerk around to see... nothing... empty blackness, nothing more. Startling me back into focus, the loud and sudden noise only serving to remind me that I am not alone, not safe. Even though Ralph seems to have vanished into thin air, and Margie is not online, I... am... not... alone.

My body is showing signs of exhaustion, losing strength, losing dexterity, becoming harder to control. The fog seems to be permeating my vision as well, blurry, double vision at times, but I keep blinking it away. I am exhausted but I couldn't sleep now if I tried, insomnia has set in. The ability to concentrate is just beyond my grasp now, sleep deprivation taking hold. Have to keep my vision clear. Must concentrate. Must complete this interface repair. Must... Keep... Moving...

As I place the final component onto the board, hands shaking, sweat running down my neck, from my hair then trickling down my back, I feel a spark of hope. If this works, it will only take a few hours to complete the repair of the damage of the ship. With Margie back in working order, she can detect the central cause, any damage caused by the blast, and guide the repairs.

Silence... In the blink of an eye, deafening silence envelopes the planet. Not a click, a drip, or a rustle. Even the fire is mute, no popping, or crackling, or sizzling. For a millisecond, I am afraid to move, to breathe, on the chance that this is the calm before an enormous, figurative storm. Quickly! I have to install this motherboard, as quickly as possible.

Leaving all the tools outside, I briskly walk into the ship, down the corridor, past the galley, then straight to the control panel. With a click and a snap, the motherboard is in place. As I reach to switch the device on, I realize that I have been holding my breath. I pause and calmly blow out the hoarded air, in one smooth relaxing breath, before pressing the button.

Control panel lights flicker at an insane pace, faster and faster, then... a hum in the system, static. In a glitchy, crackling voice, an unrecognizable chatter begins to spill from the audio speakers. Unrecognizable at first, then words start becoming clear, "Impending... detonation... Joe... stop..."

The incomprehensible chatter continues for several minutes. Then, random words repeat, which is even more confusing. Then, a whimpering sound and a pause, just before the first phrase spills from the speakers. "Good morning, Joe. Would you like coffee and breakfast?" A repeat of the first phrase spoken by Margie, when she first came online eons ago.

It is clearly her, only not her... The tone of the voice is somewhat ... off. Deeper. Raspy. Less feminine than I recall. She has been offline for who knows how long has actually passed since the ship exploded.

Time has been unpredictable in this place. Regardless, she is back. Relieved, I instruct her to do a diagnostic run on the system, the mechanics, and the framework of the ship.

"Margie, check the video of the ship for unusual activity, just before the blast took out your mainframe." The lights dim and ebb, console lights flicker, static comes from the speakers as the seconds tick away, like years. An image, badly pixelated, is trying to take shape on the console screen. Only flashes of video are coming on the screen as she searches through archived images, after several minutes have passed, Margie reports, "No unauthorized activity to report. Mechanical interfaces functioning as expected. Electrical systems stable, interface system fully online."

With each word, the voice is becoming less... Margie-like. I must be projecting my fears, because of the exhaustion. This is nonsense. I need to focus on the problem that is of the most importance, locating the damage and getting all of it in working order, so that I can return to Zenthal in one piece.

First things first, getting the ship to take us home, "Margie, pinpoint areas in need of repair and generate schematics and component lists for each repair needed."

Lights flash across the console panel. "Electrical systems functioning at peak levels. Minimal damage detected in ships port side. Minor repairs needed to reshape the hull." she reports. "Mechanical repairs needed in engine room area. Time actuator fragmented, balance wheel askew, arm shaft compromised." There is a pause in her chatter as she gathers relevant data on materials needed to effectively repair the damage. I am astonished at how little damage she is reporting. With the volume of that blast, I suspected much more devastation. It seems the most affected part of the ship was Margie.

"Compiling damage report... Instructions for repair of all damage found."

When the report was printed, I gave Margie one final directive, "Margie, determine the origin of the explosion and the underlying cause." I then set to work making the necessary repairs as indicted in her report.

In my peripheral, I am plagued with shadows shimmering in and out of my view. The whispering begins again, first to my left then shifting to my right. As I try to keep my focus on the repair process, I cannot help but feel anxious… slightly paranoid.

The voices begin again, as insistent soft whispers, then morph into a hum of muttering, but quickly rising towards a deafening volume. Incomprehensible for the most part, only shrieking, as if someone is trying to force me to listen, screaming at me, an echoing wail, as I try desperately to ignore the deafening sounds. The shadowy figures seem to be coming closer and closer with each shimmer, and I can feel the air move softly on my skin. As one rushes by, my hair stands on end, on my arms and the back of my neck.

Realizing that I have been clenching my jaw for several minutes in an attempt to fight off the shadows and the voices, and feeling the ache, I stretch my mouth open to relieve the muscles. My jaw pops loudly while stretching, and instantly… pain… unbearable pain! I frantically continue to work my jaw in hopes of relieving the burning.

I fight through the pain and following the needed repairs, then quickly gather the tools from outside, douse the fire with water while it sizzles and hisses its annoyance.

As day approaches, light peaks through the dense forest growth and the deafening silence outside of the ship begins to fade. As noises begin to emanate from the undergrowth, rustling, clicking, and slithering sounds, the day- cycle has begun.

I bring my implements into the ship and secure the door, my barrier to all that is out in the wilderness of this God forsaken planet. Returning to the control room, "Margie, report findings of causation of the explosion."

"Report complete. Video surveillance footage cued."

"Play recording."

As I watch the screen, concentrating with every cell in my being, I see a shadowy hooded image approaching the control panel. The image is familiar, but then again, not. The image is wavering and flickering. Ralph? Not Ralph, it's me! I am at the panel! No, now it is Ralph.

Wavering between the two, only slight changes in the figure morphing between the images of myself and Ralph, back and forth. What am I, is he doing? As the figure shifts to the side, an incendiary device becomes visible. It is small, but distinct.

The figure shifts once again, blocking the view of the device, but, when he turns to leave the console room... the device has been activated; a timer counting down from fifteen minutes is clearly visible.

As the figure turns his face to the camera's view... The face shimmers from my own, clean shaven and tan, to Ralph's, gaunt and pale skin and a goatee, his eyes dark and wild...

My head feels as if it is about to explode from the massive throbbing and thrumming. Then, from my left, I can make out a form, materializing next to me... Ralph! As I quickly spin to face him, he is coming at me with a baton and as I duck, it barely misses the top of my skull. He is screaming, "You have to get out! It's mine!" He looks at me with dark eyes that are wide with rage, the look of a psychopath. "You must die, so that I may live!"

"Ralph! Stop! What are you saying?!?"

"My ship!" he bellows. "I... AM... THE... ULTIMATE... TIME... TRAVELER!!" Swinging the bat at me between each word, he lashes out with the baton, connecting on the final blow. His image begins to shimmer, blur, as he attempts to get inside of my body. Then vanishing in a mist as he penetrates my psyche. I am trapped, bound, restrained by my alter-ego; Ralph has effectively infected my mind.

I Can Do Nothing to Create Wholeness

Fading in and out of consciousness, I sense that I am bound, strapped down, by my wrists and ankles. Restrained and forced to ingest an immeasurable number of, undoubtedly poison, tablets and bitter liquids, I attempt desperately to expel the poisons being forced upon me. Wavering shadows of unknown beings surround me at regular intervals, poking, prodding, and stabbing needles into my veins. Each time they come at me, I fight them; I thrash around in an attempt to escape my captors. Are they experimenting on me? Or trying to kill that small part of me that is still fighting to live? I suspect the latter of the two reasons. Will they succeed..? Blackness fades in, engulfing my conscious mind.

Dreams of the other I, my alter ego, Ralph, swinging violently at my head. Laughing like a demon, eyes glowing red, baring jagged teeth as he launches his assault. And in each dream, I raise my arms to cover my head, trying to fend off the attack, but they are smashed by the bat, every time, and I pull them away in pain.

The harder I try to defend myself, the more blows I take. My second-self is relentless. These dreams always end with a final blow to the top of my head, swimming darkness, nauseating pain, and then nothing...

A sense of light invades my vision and I fight to open my eyes. My veins are plagued with hoses, some pumping in an unknown liquid, others extracting blood. Although my panic has calmed, I feel an unbearable dread. The beings are becoming less shadowy, more humanistic, although my vision is still a bit blurry and I feel as though I am gaining strength, becoming whole. Where is Ralph and why is he not participating in this torture?

"We are here for you. The medications are beginning to take effect; you will feel much better soon." an unfamiliar voice tries to reassure me, calm me. I remain suspicious, the poisons are still pumping into me consistently and I am sure that this is just an attempt to squash any thoughts that I have of escaping. They are trying to keep me subdued, as darkness comes over me once again...

Images flood my mind of swinging arms, screaming, pain all over my body and now being held down by unseen arms. Defenseless against the assault, crying out to 'Other I' for relief... for release, rescue from this cycle of torture. Pleading with 'Second Self' to release me from this hell that I am caught in.

Excruciating pain, enormous throbbing in my head, the sting of the bat as it makes contact with my skull, agony is trying to take over my body, my mind, my soul. I beg that it ends this time, with this battle!!! End me now and free me from this endless cycle of warring halves, then once again darkness overcomes me.

As I awaken, I can feel that the restraints have been removed from my wrists. Opening my eyes, I see two faces, more clearly than my last bout of consciousness. "Do I know you?" I questioned in a raspy and unknown voice, recognizing that I know them, but unsure of how, or who they are. The woman reaches to take my hand, warm and comforting.

My unease is beginning to dissolve. I try to speak, but my mouth and throat are dry. I am so parched, I try to gulp the water that she hands me, but only gag and cough, spitting water everywhere. She reaches for a towel and attempts to sop up the water from my chest and stomach; I flinch. In a calm, soothing voice she casually says, "It's okay. I am going to gently clean up the water you spilled so you will not get a chill." After handing the refilled glass to me once again, I slowly sip the cool water before handing the glass back to her. My head feels heavy, eyelids leaden. I drift back off into darkness.

Once again I am drawn into a dream, but it is of an earlier time, a childhood battle of the selves. Alter ego, Other I, Second Self... Ralph. He is a mere juvenile, but angrier than I had recalled earlier.

As he pummels me on the ground, I reach for anything that can be used to fight him off of me. My hand curls around the edges of a cylindrical object. My fingers curl around a cold metal handle, and as I bring it into view, I see that I am holding a bat. I raise it high with the last of my strength and swing downward into the back of his head. He freezes in time, his eyes roll back into his head, a small trickle of blood coming from his nose, and then he slumps down on top of me, the weight of him almost unbearable.

I push with my hands against his shoulders, forcefully to the right, and he rolls off of me. Feeling instantly less burdened, I can breathe. All sound fades away, blurring images fade, and once again, I drift into the darkness.

I am aware, but no light penetrates my eyelids. Must be night. Opening my eyes, I see a dimmed room with the soft glow of light coming from a lamp on the table to my left. Where am I? I don't recognize this place. Using my elbows to push upward into a sitting position, I am trying to get my bearings.

I see white sheets covering my torso and legs, white tile flooring, white walls, and an aluminum bar frame to the sides of the bed that I am on. Hospital. I am in the hospital. My head is throbbing slightly so I reach up to touch my temple. Bandages. With both hands, I can feel that my entire skull has been wrapped with a bandage. I can also see cuts and scrapes on my arms and hands.

As I lift the sheet, carefully, to inspect my legs, I am pleased to see only a bit of bruising is evident. What happened to me? How did I come to be in the hospital? How long have I been here?

A nurse enters the room and proceeds to wrap a cuff around my arm, press a stethoscope against my inner elbow, and check my blood pressure. Releasing the air filled cuff and removing it from my arm, she proceeds to stick a thermometer under my tongue and holds my wrist, counting my heart rate. Without saying a word she removes then checks the thermometer, writes the levels on my chart, places my chart at the end of the hospital bed with a click, and turns to leave.

"Excuse me." I call to get her attention. She turns, "Yes, how can I help you?"

"Do you know how I got here? I mean, what happened to me?"

"You were brought in ten days ago with a head contusion, minor scrapes and bruises, fighting medical attention, and that is why you were restrained, to allow us to give you the medical attention that you need."

"Can you tell me how I got hurt? What all is wrong with me?"

"It is in your chart as a one vehicle accident and a psychiatric hold. I will inform the doctor that you are awake, lucid, and asking questions. He will be in shortly. Is there anything else?"

"Thank you, and yes. Is my mother here?"

"She is, along with your younger brother. Would you like for me to inform them that you are ready for visitors?"

"Yes, please."

Waiting with anticipation of seeing my mother and brother and letting them know that I was truly okay, I began to plan, in my head, what I would do when I get out of here. First, I would go to my cabin and check on Rooster, my white pit bull. He would be so happy to see me, he would probably knock me over. He is such a puppy, even though he is full grown. I better be braced for him so that he doesn't reinjure me.

Second on my to-do list is to check on the garden. After more than a week, I am sure it is in dire need of weeding. I hope that David, my brother, will be willing to come and help me get the weeds pulled and rows tilled. Being a teenager, you never know how he will respond to the request, though.

Surely my mother will come to help settle me back in, and maybe make a lunch. Her cooking always makes me feel better. Sliding off the side of the bed, I reach to open the curtains. A little daylight will do me good, I am sure. Wait... Is that snow? In the spring? How odd is that?

While standing at the window, an older woman and man come into my room without my hearing them. The man, looking to be in his late twenties, clears his throat to get my attention, and I turn quickly with a start. They look familiar... but, I thought my mom and bro were coming in; who are these people? The woman hesitantly takes a step towards me and almost whispers, "Andrew... Is it really you?" I am startled at the sound of her voice. It is the voice of my mom, but her hair is so gray and face wrinkled, showing that she has aged, at least into her late fifties I would guess. "Mom? What happened? You look... so... different."

The man began to speak. A deep voice but with the same inflections as... David. How has David grown up in only a week and a half? It couldn't be possible. The nurse said that I had only been here for ten days, not ten years. This is all very disturbing. Maybe I am still dreaming.

"Andy, you look very... together. I am so happy to see that you are *all here* now."

"What do you mean by '*all here*'? Aren't I always '*all here*'? And when did you become a man? Only a couple of weeks ago, you were turning seventeen and now you are a full grown man, with a beard."

Mom chimed in, "Andrew, you might want to sit down for this conversation. We might need to wait for the doctor to come in, as well." She glances over at my brother, "David, don't you think so?"

"Mom's right. The doctor will be more able to explain it all to you. We just want to make sure you are healthy, *inside and out*. He will have your charts, list of medications, and the therapist information that we will need."

I walked over to the chairs by the window and took a seat. Apparently there is more to this than a car accident. An overwhelming sense of fear starts to grip me. I can feel my breathing becoming more rapid and hear my heart beating in my head, my whole body. Whoosh whoosh, pause, whoosh whoosh, pause. It seems a bit fast for just sitting in a chair.

I start to move my hand onto my chest and I notice that it is shaking, trembling. Is this shock? Should I lay back down for this conversation? Is merely sitting going to be enough?

As my mind races through more and more questions about what is happening, the doctor strides into the room, clipboard in hand.

"Well, hello Andrew. It is nice to see you out of the bed. How are we feeling today? A bit overwhelmed, I am sure. I am Dr. Helmsley and I have been seeing to your needs while you have been here in the hospital."

"Hello, Dr. Helmsley. I have so many questions."

"I can imagine that you do. Let's start with what is in your chart… You were brought into the emergency room ten days ago, around eight o'clock in the evening. You had been involved in a one car accident in which your head struck the windshield from the impact of hitting a tree. Other than minor cuts and abrasions from shattered glass, the head trauma is the only injury of concern, physically. When you were brought in you were conscious. You were combative, fighting off the attending nurses efforts to care for your wounds. We suspected that you had ingested some illegal substance that was causing hallucinations. We did a full battery of blood tests to determine your levels of amphetamine or hallucinogen substances in your bloodstream. Much to our surprise, there were no drugs in your system."

He continued to explain my care, and why I had needed restraints, over the past week and a half. Apparently, when they brought me in, my mother was notified that I had been in an accident and to bring all prescription and medical information to the hospital.

When she arrived, she carried in a backpack of prescription bottles from insomnia meds to antipsychotic drugs. At least eight different kinds, plus papers documenting my gluten allergy and paperwork confirming my psychiatric diagnosis.

As the doctor explained my history with schizoaffective disorder, which is Bipolar disorder with a tendency for Schizophrenic episodes, the many medications and their purposes began to weave their way into my memory. I had been diagnosed at the age of nineteen, hospitalized multiple occasions for going off my medication and suffering through multiple psychotic breaks, of which I have no memory. I do however recall hearing voices and seeing shadows on occasion, even while on the medications.

When the doctor finished explaining how and why I was here, it was my turn to ask questions. "What time of year is it? I saw snow outside the window, but the last thing I remember before waking up here it was late spring and my garden plants were full of tiny fruits."

David cleared his throat and answered, "It is in mid-winter. Christmas was last week, you missed it. Your garden has... become overgrown and will need a lot of work this coming spring."

"Alright. What... year is it? The last I remember seeing *you*, David, you were barely seventeen. You are obviously NOT a teenager anymore."

Mom decided to answer this one, "Andrew, it has been nine years since David was a teenager. It has been nine years since you have been... you. You called yourself 'Joe' for many years, insisted on living alone, a hermit, and living in a cabin away from everyone in the world. I would come up and bring groceries and take care of maintenance on your... home.

David would come and take Rooster out for walks every day until he, Rooster, passed away. David and I both came up and gave him a proper burial on the mountain, so that he could stay near to you. You had gotten to the point that you would no longer go into town for doctor or therapist visits, refused medications and called them poisons, so...." she trailed off, choking back tears, and David had to continue.

"So, you weren't able to care for yourself anymore, almost completely stopped eating any foods that were prepared and only eating vegetation and fruits that you found in your wooded, mountain home area. Once, I found you eating a squirrel ... not cooked... it was raw. It was pretty disgusting, brother. Mom and I talked it over and decided for your own safety, we should have you placed in a hospital again to try and regulate your medications so that you could be Andrew, once again."

"If I was hospitalized, how did I end up in a car accident?"

The doctor gave his input on this question. He explained that during my commitment, I refused medication and had to be placed into solitary for several months. Once I had been moved into a regular room, I began to 'take' the medications and appeared to be doing much better.

I had apparently, actually been hiding the medications after pretending to take them and then flushing them down the toilet. But, I faked it enough to fool the nurses and doctors and be released back into my family's care. I moved back to the cabin and seemed to be doing okay for a little while, a few weeks, but kept insisting that I was Joe not Andrew. One day, I just walked off. Within a week, I had gotten a job and a rental car. Which leads us to the accident that resulted in my being put in the hospital.

As disturbing as what they are telling me is, the lost time, the other me, the loss of my best buddy, Rooster, I choose to accept the information I have been given, and trust that my family is looking out for me. I will go home with my mom, take the time to process all of this and get my life back. After the nightmares of the last few nights and the big knot on my head, I am convinced that the medications are necessary, for now at least, to keep the voices out of my head.

Dr. Helmsley mentioned a new medical procedure that would allow me to have more freedom, without the risk of forgetting to take my pills, or just deciding that I don't need them any longer.

As I understand it, they can place an implant in my arm, just below the skin, in the fatty layer. The implant can remain under my skin for up to five years and only requires resupplying it with all of my antipsychotic medications once each month. The medications can be time released into my bloodstream on a programmed schedule, set by the doctors, through his computer. If my dosages need adjusting, he can do it remotely from his laptop, then adjust my schedule for replacing any medications that have been adjusted. I tend to agree with Dr. Helmsley and my mother, that this is the easiest and most effective way for me to receive the medications.

Six months have passed, now, since the accident. Back at Mom's place, she has me taking care of her greenhouses, so I can resume working with my hands in the dirt. It is therapeutic, my therapist says, helps to calm the mind. Although I miss Rooster, I have found a new best buddy in the little pug puppy, Jasper, that David brought for my companionship. Mom found a used camper and David helped me set it up and get the electricity and water hooked into it. It's small, but enough for me and Jasper. Although I still hear occasional whispers late at night, when I am alone, I have seen no shadows, and I am still Andrew.

It's now early spring, one year since they put the implant in my left arm and I have been out to the cabin several times to clean it up, repair it, and to break up the garden area, getting it ready to plant.. One day, I would like to return to living on the mountain where it is peaceful and quiet, just me, Jasper, and nature. But for now, I will keep working in my mom's greenhouses, helping her with chores that are difficult for her, or that she just doesn't want to do, live in the camper behind my mom's house, and bond with Jasper. Sometimes, I think my mom is making up new stuff to do just to keep me busy...

Epilogue:

Everything That is Not Black is Not a Raven

Finally, I have come full circle, a two full years since the accident. I have just moved back into my cabin on the mountain. It's just me, Jasper, and a garden that is back to its full glory. All of the plants are growing, healthy and green, full of blooms, tiny fruits and vegetables, and hundreds of bees working in the blooms.

The sounds of nature are soothing. The sun, which has been shining through the openings in the forest ceiling to bless the garden with its warmth, is starting to fade behind the canopy of the trees. The fresh air is crisp this evening, and

I pull my jacket closer around me as a mist begins to form along the ground around the forest undergrowth just beneath the trees. Jasper is barking at a squirrel, high in the big pine out back of the cabin. I hear the flapping wings of blackbirds as they are startled by his yelping. The squirrel is sitting out on a limb, barking back at Jasper as though to say 'You can't catch me!'

Even though the air is crisp, it is laced with a salty taste, as if I were living by an ocean. Deciding it is time to get dinner on the stove, I call out to Jasper to come inside and make my way towards the backdoor of the cabin. At the edge of the forest, just outside my range of vision, a shadow ducks behind a tree. There is a familiar rustling in the leaves as I turn to focus my sight on the area. "Joe..." A rasping whisper creeps into my ears...

Reflection:

Reality Does Not Exist

As defined by the National Institute of Mental Health, Schizophrenia is a mental disorder which is characterized by disruptions in thought processes, perceptions, emotional responsiveness, and social interactions. Some of the symptoms include hallucinations, delusions, reduced expression of emotions, reduced motivation, trouble with social relationships and interactions, as well as motor and cognitive impairment. Bipolar disorder is a mental condition with alternating periods of elation and depression. When both disorders are present in an individual it is referred to as schizoaffective disorder.

Worldwide, approximately 1% of the population is diagnosed with Schizophrenia, with only .3% being schizoaffective. Although this is a very rare condition, it is a very real struggle. Mentally ill individuals are sorely underserved in the United States and laws to assist family in the management of the disorder are historically ineffective or hard to navigate.

Once an individual reaches the age of consent, 18 in the US, the family is virtually powerless to legally retain help for their affected family members, requiring that the family file with a court of law to have their family member held in jail before a judge will consider placing them in an institution for evaluation. This process is a cycle that can occur over and over for years before a court will consider granting guardianship to a family member, which allows the family member to commit them for evaluation and adjustment or reintroduction to medication without going through another court hearing.

An additional hardship for families with members who have been diagnosed with Schizophrenia or schizoaffective disorder is the cost of medications. Ziprasidone is one commonly prescribed antipsychotic medication and when first prescribed an antipsychotic medication without insurance, the brand name costed upwards of $1400 for a one month supply of 60, 80 mg capsules; which is usually only one of a list of medications prescribed to treat the disorder, with supplemental medications to help alleviate other symptoms including insomnia, tremors, diabetes, low potassium or magnesium, liver and/or kidney disease, irregular heartbeat, and other more serious possibilities.

For those who can't work because of the disorder and/or the side effects caused by medications, this is unattainable and one reason that many become street dwelling, no longer able to afford a home or medications. It seems to be an unwinnable war.

The vicious cycle of being able to get diagnosis and treatment, medication adjustments when the current levels and prescriptions are no longer effective, and walking on pins and needles with your loved one becomes the norm for many family members. Convincing them that the medications are needed, that there is truly something wrong that can be helped, that you are not poisoning them, but trying to help them is not the only struggle we face.

Watching our loved ones descend into a delusional world, become someone other than who you know them to be, paranoid and suspicious of every word you say, then not recognizing you as their family, and being powerless to stop them from self-neglect is one of the most heart wrenching parts of it.

The one thing that I really want you to understand is that for those who have mental illness, it is real. The hallucinations, the voices, the experiences that they go through in their minds is REAL to them. They feel it, the warm or cold, experience the tastes, the smells, the sounds, and the pain, possibly more vividly than reality. It is an alternate reality…

About the Author

I was born in the small town of Prescott, Arkansas, where I learned to love learning and creating. I have two grown sons, an amazing and loving mother, and three older sisters whom I admire for their deep faith in God and their love of family. After many jobs and many life trials, I have finally found my place in this world.

I now call Cove, Arkansas my home, since 2007 when I moved here to become an art teacher in a public school for K-12 students. After merging with a neighboring school district, I transitioned to the high school level with 7th through 12th grade and remained until 2019. Following the retirement of a close friend in special education, I felt a calling to transition into the special education Resource English classroom.

My extended family continues to grow including fellow teachers and students. A new journey has now begun…